Bantam Books in the Choose Your Own Adventure® Series
Ask your bookseller for the books you have missed

SPY FOR GEORGE WASHINGTON

by Jay Leibold

ILLUSTRATED BY DON HEDIN

An R. A. Montgomery Book

BANTAM BOOKS
TORONTO • NEW YORK • LONDON • SYDNEY • AUCKLAND

RL 4, IL age 10 and up

SPY FOR GEORGE WASHINGTON
A Bantam Book / September 1985

CHOOSE YOUR OWN ADVENTURE® is a registered trademark of
Bantam Books, Inc. Registered in U.S. Patent and Trademark
Office and elsewhere.
Original conception of Edward Packard

ISBN 0-553-25134-1

Published simultaneously in the United States and Canada

Bantam Books are published by Bantam Books, Inc. Its trademark, consisting of the words "Bantam Books" and the por-
trayal of a rooster, is Registered in U.S. Patent and Trademark
Office and in other countries. Marca Registrada. Bantam
Books, Inc., 666 Fifth Avenue, New York, New York 10103.

PRINTED IN THE UNITED STATES OF AMERICA

O   0 9 8 7 6 5 4

For Dick Jordan and Pat Cooney,
Manual High School, Denver, Colorado

WARNING!!!

Do not read this book straight through from beginning to end. You can have many different adventures as you attempt to deliver a vital message to George Washington in the American Revolution. As you read along you will be able to make choices. Your choices will determine whether or not you succeed in your mission.

There are many ways to get the message to Washington. You are responsible for your fate because *you* make the decisions. After you make a choice, follow the instructions to see what happens next.

Be careful! The world of a Revolutionary spy is a dangerous one. People may not always be what they seem. Good luck.

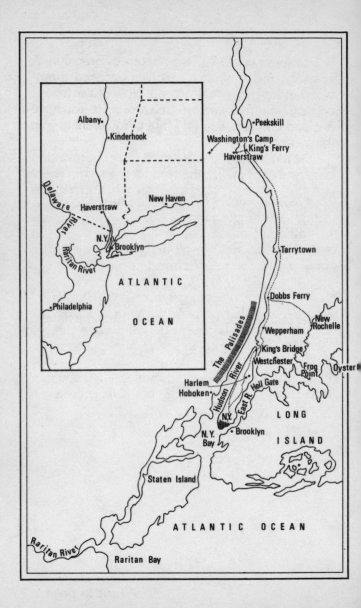

The summer of 1777 is a hot one in Brooklyn. A year ago the American colonies declared themselves independent of England. Now British troops occupy New York and the area around it. You have decided you can wait no longer. You want to join the Revolution.

One night you slip away from your chores at the farm and go down to the Red Lion Tavern. There you find your neighbor Robert Smith. You happen to know he is a rebel organizer. Smith greets you with a nod. Your families have known each other for a long time.

You must be careful no Tories overhear as you tell Smith of your resolve. These are strange times. Friends and even relatives suddenly find they are now enemies, though they continue to work together in the same town or live in the same house.

Turn to page 2.

Smith takes a long draw on his pipe and stares at the far wall as he considers your offer. "Well, we do need all the help we can get. The Revolution is at a crucial point. But I'm afraid you're just too young. The best thing you can do is keep working hard on your parents' farm, and maybe in a couple of years . . ." His voice trails off as he thinks for a moment.

"Then again," Smith says, "maybe . . ." Tugging at his whiskers, he looks at you closely before he continues. "Perhaps you would be just the right person to undertake a little mission. I was going to do it myself, but the British are already suspicious of me."

He glances around to make sure no one is listening. "General Washington is camped sixty-three miles above here, near Haverstraw on the west bank of the Hudson River. He chased the Redcoats through Jersey and back into New York City. Now he's waiting for their next move. Everyone expects the Redcoats to sail up the Hudson to Albany."

Turn to page 7.

4

"Yeee-haw!"

The scream rings out in the night. It's an ambush! Men on horseback pour from the trees.

"Marauders!" someone cries. Pistols flash in the darkness.

"Scatter!" Arzod orders. "Meet at the mansion."

You are right behind Arzod as he flees into the dark woods. He seems to know every curve of the little trail you are on, and you follow closely.

After endless twists and turns you come on to a small country lane that climbs along the side of a hill. The moon, now almost down, casts chaotic shadows through the trees. A slight breeze rustles the leaves.

The lane ends abruptly. Before you stands a dark mansion. You dismount and follow Arzod up the rickety steps to the door. Arzod opens it. You shiver as a blast of cold air hits you. He pauses in the entryway and says, "You go upstairs and check on the uniforms. I'll prepare the special weapons. The others should be here soon."

The stairs creak as you slowly walk up. Cobwebs tickle your face. At the top of the steps you stop. You can hear Arzod downstairs at the other end of the house. Clearly some sort of plan is being carried out—but in the service of what? The Crown? The Revolution? The Devil?

Go on to the next page.

You still have plenty of time to get to George Washington. Perhaps, if you are discreet, you can find out what's behind all this. However, if you want out, this may be your chance. You could dash down the stairs and take off on your horse. But you'd better watch out—the others will arrive any second.

If you go look for the uniforms, turn to page 28.

If you dash down the stairs, turn to page 22.

"Maybe you're right," you say to the spy. "I'll get some sleep tonight and start first thing in the morning."

"Good," he says. "Now I must go." He checks to make sure the coast is clear, then disappears among the burned-out buildings. As you walk back down Wall Street you glance about to make sure no one is following. Suddenly you realize you are carrying the letter openly in your hand. You tuck it in an inside pocket of your coat.

McGillicuddy is waiting for you at the wharf. "All set?" he asks.

"Yes," you say. "Can you show me where to sleep for the night?"

"Well, that would depend on whether you're goin' by land or by sea."

"By sea?"

"Didn't Smith tell you about it? You can sail up the East River, through Hell Gate, and across Long Island Sound to New Rochelle. From there you get a horse for the rest of the trip."

"Smith didn't mention it—but we were interrupted. It sounds dangerous."

"Aye—you've got the British Navy to deal with, as well as the sea itself. I wouldn't call it a pleasure cruise. But the land route would be pretty tricky, too, with the Brits watching all the roads. I can't say I know which is better. Safest place to be would be at home smokin' your pipe."

If you take the land route, turn to page 8.

If you want to go by sea, turn to page 55.

Smith lowers his voice to a murmur. "We have a spy in Manhattan who has found out otherwise. The British are going to move on Philadelphia in three days. Our spy has obtained the plans for the move, but you do not need to know the details. In fact, the less you know, the better—in case you're caught. What you need to do is get the envelope containing the plans to Washington as quickly as possible. You may be young enough to slip through British lines without attracting attention. How well do you know the Hudson?"

"I go up to Kinderhook to visit my uncle Samuel every year," you say.

"That would be the perfect cover," Smith says. "You can say you're going to visit your uncle. It just might work. It's a dangerous mission though. If they catch you . . . you'll hang." Smith regards you with arched eyebrows.

"I'll do it," you say without hesitation.

Smith tells you where to find the rendezvous point in New York City. He promises he'll tell your family you're on an important mission. Then he says, "Go down to the docks. Ask for a captain named McGillicuddy. You can trust him. He'll take you over to Manhattan, and—"

Smith frowns all of a sudden as two well-dressed men walk in the door. "Those two are Tory spies," he whispers. "You'd better go now. Good luck. And be careful."

"I'll get the envelope to Washington," you promise. You stand up and walk out the door as casually as possible.

Turn to page 11.

8

"I think I'd better take the land route," you say.

"Suit yourself," McGillicuddy says. He takes you to another rowboat moored on the dock. "Just climb in there," he says. "I'll throw this tarp over. No one will bother you. Sleep tight."

You curl up under the tarp and wait for sleep. It is important to be rested for your journey tomorrow. But your mind is racing, accompanied by the creak of the pilings and the skittering of the wharf rats. Finally the rocking water lulls you to sleep.

You awake with a start. Something is wrong— the boat is still rocking, but not gently. It is being tossed up and down by big waves. And it seems strange you can't hear any dock sounds. You fling off the tarp. You're adrift in the middle of New York Harbor without oars—and an English frigate is not far away!

Your first thought is McGillicuddy. Did he set you up for this? Then you remember what you thought was a dream—a group of drunken sailors were singing and shouting on the dock, cursing the rebels. Maybe they played a joke on you.

In any case, what's important now is that the English frigate is sailing straight for you. If they search you and find the envelope, you will be finished. Should you hide under the tarp and hope the British captain hasn't seen you? Or should you pretend you need help, and hope he believes your story?

If you hide under the tarp, turn to page 14.

If you hail the frigate, turn to page 29.

Turn to page 18

At the waterside you spot a burly sailor with red hair. "I'm looking for McGillicuddy," you say.

"Aye, that'd be me," he responds in his heavy brogue. "What would you be needing tonight?"

You tell him Smith sent you. He slaps you on the back and bellows, "Doin' a wee bit o' espionage, are ye? Well, climb aboard my rowboat. Always glad to be aidin' in the cause o' liberty. Quite a contest we're havin' here with them Brits, eh?"

You hope McGillicuddy's voice doesn't carry to the British warships anchored up the shore, but he abruptly stops talking as he starts to row you across the East River. A forest of English shipmasts looms on the other side. McGillicuddy's strong arms pull the boat swiftly across the water. It isn't long before you glide up to a Manhattan wharf.

Turn to page 15.

"I'd rather start tonight," you say.

"If you insist—but be doubly careful," the spy says. "Good luck." He disappears into the night.

The first thing you do is hide the letter inside your boot. After a stop at the docks to let McGillicuddy know you are leaving tonight, you walk up Maiden Lane to the stable. It takes several loud knocks before Ephraim is roused. He greets you at the door in his nightcap, demanding, "What do you want at this hour?"

His expression changes when you say, "I'm Culpepper."

"Come in," he says. You decline his offer of a cup of coffee, and he goes off to saddle the horse. Soon he returns. "Everything is ready outside. I've tied a saddlebag with a blanket and provisions on the horse. Good luck."

You clip-clop down the cobblestones through the sleeping city. Occasionally you turn into a side street to avoid a carousing band of British soldiers. It is only a mile to the outskirts of town, and soon you are riding through the moonlit fields and hills of rural Manhattan Island.

Go on to the next page.

The Bloomingdale Road branches to the left, but you stay with the Old Post Road on the right. A few miles on up you notice a small group of people on horseback gathered in a clearing across the way. They are clad in dark clothes with pointed hoods. As soon as they see you they disband. You wonder what strange things may be happening in the woods tonight.

Suddenly the countryside seems alive. Every snapping twig or rustling branch seems to have a secret meaning. A moment later a shadowy figure on horseback emerges from the trees ahead and hails you.

If you stop to see who it is, turn to page 39.

If you bolt on your horse, turn to page 17.

14

You duck under the tarp and wait for the British frigate to pass by. You can hear the first mate asking about your boat, but the captain says, "Let it go. We have more important things to do than worry about loose rowboats."

After a few minutes you peek out from under the tarp. There are no ships. You throw off the canvas and wonder what to do next. Wait for a friendly-looking ship, you decide.

But none come all morning. Then, around noon, a steady stream of English warships cruise by, heading for the Atlantic—preparing to sail to Philadelphia, you think.

You stay hidden under the tarp for a while, but then you realize that if you ever want to get out of the middle of the harbor, you will have to take a chance on one of the British ships.

You hail each one that passes by. They all ignore you. Not a single ship stops even to see who you might be. As darkness comes and a storm swoops in from the north, you wonder why you ever took on this mission.

The End

"I'll wait here in case you need me," McGillicuddy says with a wink. You climb out and walk up lantern-lit Wall Street to the burned-out section of town. In among the charred ruins of houses you find the rendezvous point.

"A friend of Smith's?" a voice asks.

"Yes," you say. A man in dark clothes emerges from the shadows, his eyes hidden by a hat.

"Here's the envelope," he says. "In the morning go to Ephraim's stable on Maiden Lane. Tell him your name is Culpepper. He will provide you with a horse."

You nod. He goes on: "You should leave before dawn tomorrow. But for now get some sleep. McGillicuddy will show you a safe place to sleep for the rest of the night."

"Why not leave right away?" you ask.

"I don't think that's a good idea. The British patrols are very suspicious of anyone out at this time of night. They're watching all the roads. But—it's up to you."

If you decide to sleep, turn to page 6.

If you want to go now, turn to page 12.

"I think you've got the wrong person," you say, a little bewildered, to the hooded riders.

"Are you sure?" one of them asks.

"Yes," you say. "Who's the Knight-Errant anyway?"

"Never mind," the woman says. She reins her horse around, and the group gallops off up the road. You stay where you are for a while. You want to let them get far away before you continue on.

Dawn is breaking as you reach the last British checkpoint at King's Bridge. Taking a deep breath, you approach the guard and give him your cover story.

For some reason the guard takes a dislike to you. "Going to visit your uncle, eh?" he says. "A likely story. Passage denied."

"But I must go see my uncle," you insist.

He bars the way with his bayonet. "You'll have to get a special pass from General Howe before *I'll* let you by."

You retreat from the bridge before he has a chance to harass you further. The problem now is, How will you get across the water? If you can't get across the bridge, you decide, perhaps you can go by boat.

It takes most of the day to find a farmer willing to lend you a rowboat. You leave him your horse in exchange. Finally, late in the afternoon, you cross Harlem Creek and pull up on the shore of Westchester County. You hide the rowboat in the bushes and make your way through the woods toward the road north.

Turn to page 42.

In a flash you rein your horse to the left and bolt across an open field. Looking back, you see the mysterious rider coming after you. You urge your horse on faster. After threading your way through an orchard, you come on to the Bloomingdale Road. You turn up it at full gallop. But the rider stays in close pursuit—and is getting closer!

You must do something. Ahead, a small trail takes off into the forest to the left. You swerve on to it and plunge into the dark woods. You must slow up on the downhill slope as your horse stumbles over the roots and rocks. The trail gets steeper as you go.

It ends at the bank of the Hudson River. You are at a small inlet where a stream flows into the river. Tied to a tree by the stream is a rowboat. It could be your means of escape. Should you take the rowboat across the river to the Jersey shore? Or should you cross the stream and climb the hill to your right, hoping to lose the rider in the untracked woods?

If you take the rowboat over to New Jersey, turn to page 37.

If you cross the stream and head into the woods, turn to page 91.

"Yes, death to the Knight-Errant," you say, trying not to sound too serious about it.

"Welcome, fellow Avenger," the hooded figure says. He holds up a black-gloved hand. "I am Arzod. Now come. Follow the Countess. We have far to go."

The woman in front starts up the road. It appears you have just initiated yourself into some kind of club or society. You have little choice at this point but to ride with them. Arzod hands you a black hood, which you put over your head. Then you trot on up the road behind the Avengers.

At King's Bridge the British guards stand back when you approach. "We are going to slay the Knight-Errant," the Countess announces. The guards wave you on quickly. These people, whoever they are, seem to have a lot of pull.

You cross King's Bridge and enter Westchester County as the moon sinks toward the horizon.

Turn to page 4.

The Countess comes back down the hallway and pokes her head into the room.

"Tell them I'll be right down," you say.

"Hurry!" she says.

Outside you find a gleaming four-horse carriage. The Countess is in the coach, along with Arzod—who has turned into a French count, powdered wig and all.

Go on to the next page.

One of the men dressed as a soldier has your horse. You mount up and fall into line in front of the carriage.

The procession makes good time up the Hudson toward Haverstraw. As you draw closer to the American lines people come out to cheer when you pass. Arzod waves his handkerchief.

Turn to page 24.

You run down the stairs two steps at a time, burst out the door, and jump onto your horse. You give it a kick and it gallops down the road, away from the mansion.

But you get only a quarter of a mile before you run into the rest of the party. You rein up quickly and try to think of an explanation.

"I—uh . . . I dropped something back there," you say.

They look confused. You give your horse a kick and turn into the woods to get around them, but a tree branch knocks you out of the saddle.

"Aagh!" you cry in pain. "My leg!"

The others rush to your side. One of them feels your leg and says, "It's broken. We'd better get you back to the mansion."

Arzod sets your leg in a homemade splint. Through the pain you are hazily aware they are leaving you at the mansion.

"We have no time to lose," Arzod says. "But we will come back for you—after we have finished with the Knight-Errant."

At least your attempt to flee did not give you away. But you still do not know what these people are up to. What's worse, there is little chance you will be able to get your message to George Washington.

The End

You go downstairs to search for the letter. Maybe by retracing your steps last night, you will find some clue to where it might be.

A few early patrons are having breakfast. You check the table where you had supper. Nothing. You look around the innkeeper's desk. Nothing. You go to the fireplace—and there, on the mantel, sits the letter, intact. Then you remember—you took it out, just for a minute, to dry it off. In your exhaustion you must have left it there. You can't believe you were so careless!

Well, what matters is that you have the letter safely in hand. You skip breakfast and immediately hit the road. The rain has passed, and it's a bright sunny day. You take a ferry across the Hudson before noon, and by two you are waiting outside General Washington's tent. You are a little worried about the letter—what if it turns out to be some kind of hoax?

Turn to page 26.

A barge is waiting at King's Ferry to take you across the Hudson. In Haverstraw, Alexander Hamilton, General Washington's aide-de-camp, greets the couple in the carriage with a smart salute.

"Count and Countess de Trompereau, it is my privilege to welcome you in the name of George Washington and the American Army," Hamilton says. "After all our correspondence it is a pleasure to meet you at last. If you will follow me, the general is waiting to receive you."

This, you think, is getting strange.

Hamilton leads the Count and his retinue—which includes you—along the road to General Washington's camp. All along the way soldiers cheer your procession. You wonder how Arzod and the Countess have been able to pull off such a feat of deception.

A half hour later you arrive. A twelve-gun salute greets you. George Washington is waiting outside his tent. You have a feeling the moment of decision has arrived. Should you expose the Avengers? You wonder if anyone would believe your story about them.

*If you decide to expose the charade,
turn to page 32.*

*If you resolve to keep a close eye on the
Avengers instead, turn to page 52.*

The Countess comes back into the room and says, "What is it?"

"Well, I just wanted to make sure I've got the plan right," you say. "What happens next?"

"What happens next?" she repeats impatiently. "We ride up the Hudson and walk right into Washington's camp."

"Yes, of course," you say, as the connections light up in your mind. "Washington is the Knight-Errant!"

"Well, of course—" She breaks off and comes closer to look you over. "Who *are* you anyway?" A small pistol appears in her hand. "Impostor!"

She marches you outside, where Arzod, dressed as a French count, is waiting in a carriage. The rest are on horseback in their fake American Army uniforms.

"We have a traitor in our midst," she announces, pushing you into the carriage.

Arzod looks at you in surprise. "I *thought* there was something strange going on. But since you knew all the passwords . . ."

As the carriage lurches into motion you say, "I have just one question. What was with all the hoods and funny talk?"

"I suppose it wouldn't hurt to tell you," the Countess says, "since you won't be around to repeat it. It was to keep snoopers away. We figured no one would want to tangle with a coven of witches and warlocks. Once we have George Washington in our hands," she adds, "you miserable revolutionaries will get what's coming to you!"

Turn to page 34.

An aide shows you into the general's tent. Washington stands to receive you. You are surprised at his height and his gangly limbs—they seem to go in all directions at once.

"You have a message for me?" he asks.

"Yes," you say hesitantly, "but I'm not sure it's . . . real."

Washington opens the envelope. He laughs when he reads the letter. "It's for my old friend Hogglebottom," he explains, taking a bottle of clear fluid from the desk drawer. He motions for you to come around the desk.

You watch as he brushes the liquid over the entire letter. A new message appears underneath the letter to Hogglebottom.

General Washington looks over the British plans to move on Philadelphia with satisfaction. He turns to you and says, "I take it you've never seen invisible ink?"

The End

Whatever is going on, it is intriguing enough to stay—at least for a little while longer. You head upstairs as the light of dawn begins to filter through the fogged windows.

In one of the rooms you find a closet full of blue uniforms—the uniforms of the American Army. The door slams downstairs, and you hear the rest of the group, having eluded the brigands, coming up to join you.

"Ah, so you've found the uniforms," the Countess says as she pulls off her hood. She goes into another room and the rest come in and don the uniforms hurriedly.

There is one more uniform, so you decide you'd better follow their lead. You quickly put it on after the rest have gone downstairs. A moment later the Countess looks in on you—only now she really looks like a French countess. Her hair is piled high and her silk dress glitters with jewels.

"Are you ready?" she asks. "Everyone is waiting downstairs. It's a long way to Haverstraw." She starts down the hallway.

"Wait!" you call after her. You have a thousand questions, like who the Knight-Errant is and what the uniforms are for and why she is dressed as a countess. But maybe it is not the right time to reveal any sign of ignorance.

If you say, "I have a question,"
turn to page 25.

If you say, "Tell them I'll be right down,"
turn to page 19.

You play it cool and hail the frigate when it pulls up.

"What are you doing on these waters?" the captain demands.

"I'm stranded," you reply as innocently as possible.

They bring you on board and you start to explain to the captain how a bunch of drunken sailors set you adrift without oars, but he cuts you short. "Tell it to Colonel Purt at New York headquarters," he says, "because that's where we're taking you."

Colonel Purt is a lean, severe-looking man with a sharp nose.

"What's the problem here?" he demands of the guards who bring you into his office. You notice he has a fire going in the grate, which seems strange on this summer morning.

They explain that you were found floating in New York Harbor "to no apparent purpose."

"I was just—" you start.

"Search this person," the colonel orders his aide, ignoring your attempt to speak. You start getting scared. They will surely find the envelope.

You stand helplessly as the aide rifles through your pockets. The envelope is the first thing he finds. You watch as he sets it, along with the rest of your things, on the colonel's desk.

If you try to spring for the letter and throw it in the fire, turn to page 50.

If you act calm and hope for the best, turn to page 36.

The next day you are loaded on to a prison transport bound for Boston. "We want to keep the crazies away from General Washington," the stockade captain explains to you. You have heard no word about the outcome of the Count and Countess de Trompereau's visit, and no one will answer your questions.

The court-martial never takes place. Languishing in the Boston prison, you can only wonder where you went wrong.

The End

"Wait!" you cry to Alexander Hamilton. "Don't let these people in! They're impostors!"

Hamilton turns and looks down his long, aquiline nose at you. "Good heavens, do you know what you are saying? Are you crazy?"

"Yes—I mean, no—" you say breathlessly. "It's some sort of plot . . . I'm not exactly sure what they're up to . . . we went to a mansion and put on these disguises—"

"Take this soldier away," Hamilton orders his guard, "as far away as possible!"

As you are dragged away, still protesting, you can hear Hamilton apologizing to the phony Count.

They throw you in the stockade. "I must see General Washington!" you insist. "I have an urgent message for him. The British are going to move on Philadelphia!"

The captain in charge looks at you with mock sympathy. "Everyone knows the British are going for Albany," he says. "And as for seeing General Washington, just be patient. You'll get your chance at the court-martial."

You have one last resort—the letter itself. You extract it from your boot and thrust it through the bars. "Here. This will prove my credentials."

Go on to the next page.

The captain takes the envelope skeptically. He opens it, reads the contents, and hands it back to you with a derisive laugh. "I don't know who Hubert Hogglebottom is, but I don't think George Washington will be very interested in him."

You look at the contents of the letter. It is addressed to someone named Hubert Hogglebottom, telling him his order for two suits of clothing will not be available for some time. It is signed *Hercules Mulligan*.

Maybe you *are* going crazy!

If you think you must try to escape at all costs, turn to page 41.

If you decide to wait for the court-martial because you're sure your name will be cleared, turn to page 31.

The Count and Countess, or whoever they really are, drop you off at a Tory merchant's house. They say they'll deal with you later.

You are left bound and gagged in the Tory's sitting room. In just a few hours the plot to assassinate George Washington will go into action—and there is nothing you can do about it.

A maid comes into the room. She closes all the doors and comes over to you. "I heard those people say you are working for the rebels. So am I," she says, revealing a vial containing a green liquid. "This will knock out my master. Then I can release you."

You nod vigorously and hope she can pull it off. A half hour later she returns with a kitchen knife and cuts your bonds.

"He's out cold," she says. "He'll wake up in a few hours and never know what hit him. Now I'll go get you a fast horse."

You thank her profusely, hop on the horse, and gallop away to warn George Washington.

The End

36

You watch as the colonel looks over your belongings. He picks up the envelope and opens it. You feel numb. After he has read it, Colonel Purt returns the letter to its envelope and fingers the rest of your things. You wait for the verdict.

"What were you doing in the harbor?" he asks at last.

"I . . . I fell asleep in my boat, and someone untied it," you answer as truthfully as you can.

He looks you over once more. "You seem harmless enough," he says. "You may go."

You can't believe it. You try to keep a straight face as the aide flings your belongings back in your lap. You nervously stuff them into your pockets.

Out on the street, in the bright sunshine, you pull out the letter and read it. The letter *does* seem harmless! It is addressed to *Hubert Hogglebottom, Esq.*, and it informs him that his order for two suits of clothing will not be available for some months. It is signed *Hercules Mulligan,* a Broad Street tailor.

You stare at the letter in a daze. Is it a code? Is it a joke?

Turn to page 40.

You jump off your horse and grab the saddlebag. You give the horse a slap on the rump, hoping it will find its way home and divert your pursuer along the way. Then you untie the rowboat and drag it to the water. Once you get the oars in the oarlocks, you are able to pull swiftly away from the shore.

You row steadily across the Hudson. It is almost two miles to the opposite bank. You bring the rowboat on shore to a narrow strip of woods between the river and a cliff looming above you. The cliff is part of the Palisades, a wall of rock that stretches all the way to the New York border.

Now that you are in New Jersey, you reflect on your situation. You do not know the territory well. You have only a vague picture of the roads and terrain. It is wilder than the route you were planning to take. But, you think, as you lay out your blanket for sleep, at least you've crossed the Hudson. And there should be less interference on this side from the British—and others.

Turn to page 47.

Cautiously you approach the figure on horse-back. The black hood covering the rider's eyes makes you shiver.

"God save the King," a woman's voice says from behind the hood.

"God save the King," you reply, playing it safe.

Several more figures emerge from the woods behind you. A man behind you says, "Shall we go to the Knight-Errant and cut off his head? For he has strayed from the path." It sounds almost like an incantation. Is this some kind of cult? you wonder. Who is the Knight-Errant? What should you say?

If you play along with them and say, "Yes, death to the Knight-Errant," turn to page 18.

If you say, "I think you've got the wrong person," turn to page 16.

Whatever the case, you decide, the only thing to do is complete your mission as planned and hope General Washington can solve this riddle.

Already you have lost the morning with Colonel Purt's questioning. You'd better get moving. First you go to Ephraim's stable for a horse and tack. Then you make your way through the alleys of the East Side to Bowery Lane, past a few stray cattle, and on to the Old Post Road. The fragrant green meadows and rolling hills of Manhattan Island, laced with streams and lakes, surround you. A group of British soldiers are playing cricket in a field.

By late afternoon you pass the road to the little Dutch town of Harlem and ride on across the Harlem Plain. When you reach the tip of the island, threatening thunderheads are gathering in the north. But you push on. So far your luck has held.

Turn to page 49.

The stockade looks pretty rickety. You wait until the captain is occupied with other matters, then go to work on the bars of your back window. With a good bit of pulling and kicking they come loose. Checking once more to make sure the captain is distracted, you tear out the bars and exit through the window.

You race to George Washington's tent. Knowing you will never get in by the front way, you sneak around to the back and slip through a fold in the canvas. You come in right behind the Count, who is standing behind General Washington. The Count raises his arm. Instinctively you leap on him. The two of you crash to the ground. You wrestle away the object in his hands as the others in the tent rush to break up the fight. The general takes the Count's weapon from you.

"A dagger!" he exclaims. "What's the meaning of this?"

Turn to page 45.

You reach the edge of the woods and pause to see if the road is clear. A commotion in the bushes behind you causes you to turn around. A black man in tattered clothes, gasping for breath, stops in his tracks as he catches sight of you. For a moment you stare wide-eyed at one another.

He breaks the silence. "I won't lie to you. My name is John, and I'm a runaway slave. The British captured me and forced me into their army. But I escaped from them too. Now there's a manhunt. Seems like the whole British Army is after me." He pauses to see your reaction.

"I won't lie to you either," you say. "I want to keep as far away as I can from the British Army."

"Well," he says, "I figure on heading north, to the American lines. I want to get in on this Revolution. Want to join forces?"

Suddenly both of your heads jerk up at the sound of baying bloodhounds. You can see the British dragnet coming out of the woods on the other side of the road. It is heading straight for you!

If you want to join forces with John, turn to page 44.

If you think you'd be safer traveling alone, turn to page 89.

"We're partners," you say to John. "Now, let's get out of here!"

You start to head north, but John grabs your arm. "No—not that way! There's another search party coming from the north. We should go south first, then double back around."

John takes off to the south and you follow. You push swiftly through the dense forest, but no matter how hard you run, the bloodhounds are never far behind.

"Wait a minute," you say, stopping to catch your breath. "We'll never be able to outrun those dogs. We have to get them off our scent. Why don't we go to the river and swim a ways downstream?"

"Good idea," John agrees.

You strike west to Harlem Creek and take off your boots. Then you jump into the water, holding your boots above the surface. A log floats by, and you and John grab on to it and let it carry you downstream. Ten minutes later you pull yourselves out of the water.

"Listen," John says, smiling. "No dogs."

You travel cross-country over the rugged hills of the Bronx, fording the Bronx River to get to the road that goes to the town of Westchester.

"Now we head north," John says. "We should be able to slip around the search parties and go on up to the American lines."

You make good time walking through the night. By suppertime the next day you have put the envelope into George Washington's hands, and John has found his freedom.

The End

The rest of the Count's group turn on the patriots. You join in the fray, and soon they are under control. The Count, restrained by several of General Washington's aides, spits out at him, "Traitor! Infidel! Barbarian!"

Suddenly you realize who the Knight-Errant is.

When things have calmed down a bit, you get up the nerve to show George Washington the letter. He takes one look at it and laughs. "Ah! It's for my good friend Hogglebottom. That means," he says, taking a bottle of clear liquid from his desk, "we'll just apply a little of this, and—*voilà!*" You watch, amazed, as the liquid develops the invisible ink underneath the Hogglebottom letter, revealing the British plans to invade Philadelphia.

The End

You wake up in the morning with a frightening sight staring you in the face. Fierce eyes, bright gashes of color across the cheeks and forehead, and a single eagle feather set in a narrow strip of hair down the middle of an otherwise bare head— it's a Mohawk!

With a scream you jump up and dash through the woods. Quickly you come up against the rock wall of the Palisades, but fright takes you where your feet normally couldn't go. You find a steep gully in the cliff and scramble up, not daring to look down as you go higher and higher. Near the crest you hear a howl. You look up to see a pack of wolves waiting at the top. One of them licks his chops.

Which will it be—down to the Mohawk or up to the wolves?

If you go back down, turn to page 83.

If you keep climbing, turn to page 94.

Night comes, the cannon fire lets up, and you quietly move toward the *Tremulous*. The darkness is complete as clouds cover the moon. Finally the storm lets loose, pouring down thick sheets of rain punctuated by bolts of lightning.

"All the better," McGillicuddy says. "They won't expect anything in this kind of weather. Long as we don't get thrown over by the waves."

Every time lightning flashes, you look for the *Tremulous* to memorize its position so you can move in on it. McGillicuddy, fighting the rain and wind, manages to pull up close to the warship.

"It seems pretty quiet on deck," you say. "Maybe they're all below, keeping dry."

McGillicuddy waits for a flash of lightning to illuminate the deck. "You're right," he says. "I bet they're nappin'. We could do some pretty good damage to them with our swivel gun—maybe even get close enough to hit the magazine and blow 'er sky-high."

"Heck," says one of the crew, "why don't we go on board? We'll lock 'em all down below, and the ship'll be ours!"

If you choose to board the Tremulous, *turn to page 81.*

If you decide to attack with the swivel gun, turn to page 68.

You make it past King's Bridge, the last British outpost, with the help of your cover story about visiting your uncle. You are in Westchester County now. You must be careful. The Hudson Valley is a hotbed of fierce Tory-rebel feuds.

Just outside Wepperham the storm finally bursts on you. A driving rain turns the road to mud, and thunder rumbles through the valley. You stop at the Wepperham Inn. It looks safe enough, and you want to get dry. You leave your horse in the stable and go in out of the rain.

As you sign in with the innkeeper a familiar name jumps out at you from the logbook. Hubert Hogglebottom, Esq., is staying at the Wepperham Inn tonight! Should you confide in him? Perhaps he can solve the mystery of the letter. Or would it be better to keep it to yourself?

If you decide to keep the letter to yourself,
turn to page 54.

If you want to talk to Hogglebottom,
turn to page 73.

You gather all your strength and spring for the colonel's desk. You grab the letter and toss it into the fire. The flames consume it quickly.

The colonel, who has half risen from his seat, loses his composure for only a moment. He sits down again, purses his lips, and says quietly, "I'd say you have just exposed yourself as a spy."

You say nothing. You have failed in your mission, but at least you have prevented the Redcoats from discovering the secret message for Washington. Now you fear what punishment may face you.

"The gallows?" the aide eagerly asks the colonel.

"No," he sighs. "This spy is too young to hang. Besides, the evidence is gone. Off to the brig with this one."

The End

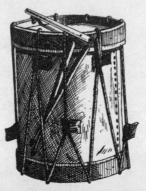

You feel you have no way out but to face down Hogglebottom. "Ha," you scoff, "I'd like to see *you* in a duel."

Hogglebottom calms himself, picks up the pieces of the letter, and stalks out the door. You follow, and behind comes a curious crowd.

Outside Hogglebottom suddenly turns and wrestles you to the ground. You are trapped, gasping, beneath his great bulk. He whispers in your ear, "Run up to your room. I'll meet you up there after I get rid of this crowd."

Since Hogglebottom has the letter, you have little choice but to follow his instructions. He rolls off you. You dash through the crowd, run up the stairs, and slam your door behind you.

A half hour later a knock comes at your door. Cautiously you let Hogglebottom in. He sits down, lets out a long breath, and begins to explain.

"You must excuse my behavior," he says, "but it was foolish of you to bring out that letter with so many Tory ears about. I have a reputation to preserve as the staunchest Tory in the valley. It is that reputation which allows me to undertake so much valuable intelligence work for General Washington. So you see, we are actually comrades-in-arms."

You stare open-mouthed. It is hard to believe this fat businessman is really a patriot spy.

"Do not be surprised," he says with a laugh. "My appearance is my best cover. Now, you'd better be on your way. Perhaps George Washington will be able to explain the letter to you"

The End

You decide to keep a close eye on the Count and his retinue.

With great pomp and circumstance Hamilton introduces "our special friends from France." Washington bows deeply and kisses the hand of the Countess.

"Won't you please come in?" he says to the phony French aristocrats.

You and the others disguised as American soldiers, as well as General Washington's guard, follow them inside. After many proclamations of goodwill and support for the Revolution, accompanied by numerous toasts, the general turns to take a bottle of champagne from his cabinet. You see the Count give a subtle nod to his companions.

You dive across the room and tackle Washington. At the same instant the Countess lifts a blowgun to her lips and fires a dart. It passes over your head and hits one of her men, who sinks to the ground. A general brawl follows, but soon the de Trompereaus and their fellow conspirators are subdued and led away.

Once everyone has recovered from the shock, George Washington shows his gratitude by giving you a dinner, attended by all his highest officers and best friends. Not only have you brought him news of the British move—you have saved his life!

The End

54

You don't ask about Hogglebottom. The fewer people who know about your mission, you decide, the better.

After drying off in front of the fire in the main room, you have a hot supper and retire to your room upstairs. You make sure your door is securely locked and climb into bed.

At dawn you wake up. Instinctively you reach for your coat by the bed. The letter is gone!

A frenzied search of the room turns up nothing. You check the door—it's still locked.

If you search downstairs, turn to page 23.

If you question the innkeeper, turn to page 59.

"I'll take the sea route," you say. "Where can I find a captain with a boat?"

McGillicuddy pauses a moment before saying, "You're lookin' at him."

"Oh!" you exclaim. "Where's your boat?"

"It's docked over at Brooklyn. I've got a whaleboat, a twenty-six-footer with a nifty swivel-gun in front. Let's head back. You can catch some sleep on the boat, and I'll round up the crew."

Before dawn you are on your way up the East River in the battered old whaleboat, named the *Margaret*. A wind begins to rise, and McGillicuddy hoists sail so the crew of eight can take a rest from rowing.

"If anyone stops us," McGillicuddy says, "I'll just explain we're going to New Rochelle to pick up a load of whale oil. And," he adds with a wink, "we are too. Course I won't tell 'em we have an extra passenger on board."

Turn to page 60.

56

"Full speed ahead!" you cry. The *Margaret* swings into position and heads for Hell Gate. But a moment later another obstacle appears—a British warship!

McGillicuddy looks at the warship through the spyglass and says softly, "Oh me, oh my. I recognize that one. It's the *Tremulous*. She's a big one. Let's just hope she doesn't want to bother us small fry."

"Can we turn back?" you ask.

McGillicuddy looks behind. "Too late now. No room to turn around. We're going through." To his crew he shouts, "Have your pistols and cutlasses ready, lads, just in case them Brits give us any trouble."

McGillicuddy skillfully maneuvers the *Margaret* through Hell Gate's reefs. The rushing current grabs the boat, and you shoot through the gap. At the same time the British ship comes about and pulls back from the Gate.

Suddenly tongues of flame leap from the side of the *Tremulous,* followed by loud cracks and rumbling.

"That's not thunder," you cry. "It's cannon fire!"

Go on to the next page.

The warship is now headed out toward Long Island Sound, and you follow behind, keeping your distance. When you round Frog's Point and come into the Sound, you see the object of the cannon fire: an American schooner, running for its life. You've stumbled into a naval battle! A shout comes up from the crew. They want to join in the fight.

"I'm not one to pass up a good fight," McGillicuddy says. "But we could also try to slip around in back of the Brits and hope they leave us alone. What do you think we should do?"

You're tempted to help the American schooner —and you may not be able to slip past the *Tremulous,* anyway. But should you delay your mission?

If you join in the fight, turn to page 69.

If you try to slip behind the British ship, turn to page 64.

58

You lift the edge of the table and push it over in one swift motion. It knocks Hogglebottom backward into his chair, which collapses under his weight. The table lands on his foot, and he lets out a yowl. You grab the two pieces of the letter and dash out of the tavern. Several diners rise from their seats, but they are too stunned to pursue.

In the stable you look desperately for your horse. The first one you see is a strong-looking mare. The initials H. H. are carved on the saddle in the stall. Why not? you think.

You burst out of the stable astride Hogglebottom's horse and into the dark, wet night. The driving rain feels good on your face after the stifling atmosphere of the Wepperham Inn.

Turn to page 65.

You find the innkeeper in the kitchen and question him about your missing letter. You tell him your room has been robbed and demand to know who has keys to the rooms. He insists he is the only one with a key and knows nothing about any letter.

Despairing, you go to search the rest of the tavern. Just as you enter the main room, you see a man in a tricornered hat by the fireplace. He is reading something that looks just like your letter.

You stride up to him and say, "Hey, that's my letter!"

He narrows his eyes at you. "Is that a fact? And what would you be doing taking a letter to that lousy Tory, Hubert Hogglebottom?" A crowd gathers around you. "We don't like your type," the man says. "We don't like Tories. We have a special treatment for them."

"The dunking stool! The dunking stool!" cries the crowd.

You protest it's really a letter for George Washington.

"And I'm really the King of England," the man replies.

Turn to page 63.

It is afternoon when you reach the top of the East River and make a turn to the northeast. Ahead lies Hell Gate—a narrow chute of swirling currents and treacherous reefs greatly feared by sailors. Once you get through it, you'll be able to go on out past Frog's Point and into Long Island Sound.

As you draw closer to Hell Gate, McGillicuddy starts to mutter to himself. "I don't like it," he says under his breath, squinting at the northern horizon.

You look to the north and see a big thunderhead gathering. McGillicuddy keeps muttering, so finally you ask if the storm clouds are bothering him.

"Weather might get bad," he says. "Wouldn't want to get caught in a storm in Hell Gate. That'd be the end of us."

"Should we hold back?" you ask.

"Hard to say," he replies. "If we could get through now, before the storm, it might be our only chance for a while. On the other hand we could head a little ways up the Harlem River, drop anchor, and try to wait out the storm."

The ship rounds a point, and Hell Gate comes into view. A loud rumbling comes across the water. McGillicuddy is leaving the decision to you.

If you tell McGillicuddy to go full speed for Hell Gate now, turn to page 56.

If you tell him to pull back and turn up the Harlem River, turn to page 82.

You are in the grip of the mob. They take you out to Wepperham Pond, tie you to the dunking stool, and prepare to hoist you out over the water. But first, the rebel throws the letter in the water.

You spend several intervals of time under the water, to the great amusement and applause of the crowd. Finally they tire of their sport and release you. You fish out the soggy letter.

With relief you retrieve your horse and hightail it out of Wepperham. Outside town, after making sure no one is around, you take out the letter to dry it out. But it is too late. The ink has run, and nothing is left but a big indecipherable blob.

The End

"Let's try to slip behind the *Tremulous*," you say to McGillicuddy.

McGillicuddy pilots the boat around to the left, hugging the shore and keeping as much distance as possible between you and the English ship. But the *Tremulous* comes about and trains its cannon on you. The balls whiz across the water and splash all around you.

"Heave to!" McGillicuddy cries. The *Margaret* backs out of range of the cannon. The *Tremulous* returns its attention to the American schooner. But every time you try to move out and get by, the British ship turns and prevents your passage.

"She's not going to let us by," McGillicuddy concludes. "We'll just have to wait until the schooner draws her away—or until night."

Turn to page 67.

Early in the morning the storm lets up. In a few hours you are sitting before General Washington, who laughs when he hears your story and reads the letter addressed to Hogglebottom. "Good old Hoggle," he says, "always playing the part to the hilt."

You want to know more, but the general refuses to tell. "There is only one person other than me who knows Hogglebottom's true identity. Don't worry about your encounter with him—he'll understand."

Washington then removes a bottle of clear fluid from his desk. "Have you ever seen invisible ink?" he asks.

Turn to page 79.

Night comes—and with it finally comes the storm from the north. It hits with sudden ferocity. The wind whips the sea into a caldron of whitecaps and the rain lashes the *Margaret*. McGillicuddy struggles desperately to keep her under control. He drops sail and manages to edge into a protected inlet, but a huge wave rolls over the bow and knocks him to the deck. The boat yaws wildly. You rush to his side.

McGillicuddy is out! You must take the helm of the *Margaret*. Fortunately you have a little bit of sailing experience from occasional fishing expeditions around Brooklyn. It takes every bit of luck and skill for you to keep the boat from capsizing.

You are almost unaware of the passing hours as you concentrate on your task. The rain finally stops sometime late in the night, but the wind is still strong and the sea is choppy.

Daylight is coming soon, you realize. You must decide whether to make your move now—while you still have cover of darkness—in an adverse wind and with an exhausted crew. Your other choice is to stay in the protected inlet and hope calm waters come in time for you to slip by the *Tremulous*.

If you move out now, turn to page 96.

If you hold off as long as possible, turn to page 84.

McGillicuddy gets the *Margaret* into position, and you fire on the *Tremulous*. It takes a while for the *Tremulous* to respond, but finally the crew mans the guns and begins to fire back at you. You trade fire in the raging storm and take numerous hits. At last the storm gets so bad, you have to lay off.

That gives you a chance to survey the damage. The *Margaret* is in tatters. The masts are splintered into pieces, and the deck is littered with wreckage. You figure the *Tremulous* must be in pretty bad shape too. You can hear the crewmen calling to one another as they try to put out fires and pump the bilge.

A heavy fog moves in at daylight. There is little you can do but paddle feebly with what bits of wood are left. It is hard to tell which way you are going in the fog. You don't know where the *Tremulous* is—but they don't know where you are either. There is no sign of the schooner, so you assume it escaped in the fog. You can only hope land appears soon.

All of a sudden the boat shakes and shudders. Everyone scans the water.

Turn to page 78.

"We can't just abandon the American schooner," you say. "We've got to help."

"Heave to, boys!" McGillicuddy cries to the crew. "We're going to join in the fight!"

You set an easterly course for the scene of the action. As you draw closer you notice the *Tremulous* has the American schooner trapped in Oyster Cove.

Turn to page 71.

The cannons roar mercilessly on the schooner, and the Americans return fire just as fiercely. A dense curtain of smoke hangs over the water, bringing the smell of gunpowder.

Go on to the next page.

"Should we try to get past the *Tremulous* and go straight into the cove?" you ask McGillicuddy.

"Aye, we could try that. The question is, Do we want to? Maybe we should wait until nightfall. Then we could sneak up behind the Brits and possibly do them some real damage."

On the other hand by nightfall you may be too late to help the schooner.

If you make for Oyster Cove, turn to page 77.

If you wait to move under cover of darkness, turn to page 48.

"Could you tell me who Mr. Hogglebottom is?" you ask the innkeeper.

"There is the gentleman now, coming down the stairs."

You turn to see a florid man with a large back-side and a rather stiff manner of walking—or wad-dling—come off the stairs and take a table for supper. He is an imposing figure. You take a deep breath and approach his table.

"Mr. Hogglebottom?" you ask politely.

"Yes," he sniffs. "I am Hubert Hogglebottom." He pronounces his name thickly, as if his tongue is in the way.

"I think I may have some business with you," you say, glancing about to see if anyone is listening.

He makes an impatient gesture for you to sit down. You carefully take out the letter and hand it to him. He places his spectacles on his nose and begins to read.

You whisper, "Do you know if General Washington—"

Go on to the next page.

"I do not know this person!" Hogglebottom bursts out. To your horror he rips the letter in half. "This is vile forgery! It is an outrage! It—it—" he sputters. He stands up, veins popping out on his forehead, spectacles tumbling to the floor.

Reaching for the torn letter, you take the opportunity to say, "I'm sorry, I must have made a mistake—"

He grabs the letter and narrows his eyes. "Did you say something about Washington? That scoundrel, that rabble-rouser, that blight upon His Majesty's empire! How dare you implicate me with him!" He crumples the two pieces of the letter and throws them to the ground. By now every face in the room is turned toward you.

"I demand satisfaction!" Hogglebottom proclaims, pounding the table. "I challenge you to a duel!"

*If you try to make a fast getaway,
turn to page 58.*

*If you decide to accept Hogglebottom's
challenge, turn to page 51.*

Carefully avoiding any mention of your secret mission, you try to explain to M that you can't go to an English hospital.

But M insists on taking you to Staten Island. "They have the best medicine for your people."

"I don't like the British," you finally say.

After you say this, something seems to dawn on M. He calls his companions together. They confer in their canoes in the middle of the river. When it is over, M says, "You will be our captive. We are allies with the English. You must be a valuable captive if you so much do not want to see them."

Your heart sinks. "Are you going to turn me over to the English?" you ask.

"No," M says, "you are *our* captive. You will come back to our village. There we will receive great honor for capturing an enemy warrior!"

For a week you travel toward Indian territory, first to Staten Island, then down through Raritan Bay and up the river. You have no opportunity to escape. The country gets hillier and the people fewer as the Mohawks paddle along.

A hazy dawn comes over the Raritan River on your eighth day of captivity. With resignation you get on the water for another day of travel. But then something blue catches your eye in the bushes on the riverbank. You look again. A group of men in blue are standing there. They must be American soldiers! This could be your last chance to escape.

If you capsize the canoe to try to escape, turn to page 107.

If you call out to the soldiers, turn to page 93.

The *Margaret* makes for Oyster Cove. You will try to squeeze between the *Tremulous* and the coast to go to the aid of the schooner. The smoke from the cannon fire will give you some cover.

But the smoke clears at just the wrong moment. Suddenly you are exposed. The *Tremulous* is only a few hundred feet away. It turns, aims, and fires.

The first cannonball smashes directly into the bow of the *Margaret*. You don't even have time to return fire. A rain of cordage and timbers comes down on you as the whaleboat is torn to pieces. The barrage does not let up until the *Margaret* is sunk. You go down with the ship.

The End

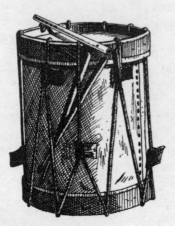

"Over there!" cries one of the crew.

Something big and dark is coming up from under the surface. It's a whale!

In the debris around your feet you find a harpoon. You pick it up.

"You're crazy," McGillicuddy says when he sees what you mean to do: to harpoon the whale so it will take the *Margaret* away like a horse drawing a carriage.

Maybe he is right. Maybe it is better to drift and stay alive, even if you must risk meeting up with the British, than to put yourself at the mercy of a whale.

If you aim the harpoon at the whale, turn to page 86.

If you lay down the harpoon and paddle for land, turn to page 85.

"No," you say.

"Of course not," he says, laughing. "It's invisible." He brushes the liquid over the pieced-together letter, and—as if by magic—the British plans to invade Philadelphia appear underneath the letter to Hogglebottom.

You've done such a good job that Washington asks if you want to join his intelligence service. You jump at the chance. Soon you are on your way to Philadelphia to set up an intelligence network for the arrival of the Redcoats.

The End

It takes a lot of nerve to board a British warship with only a whaleboat crew. "Let's do it!" you say.

McGillicuddy pulls the *Margaret* in until it bumps up against the *Tremulous*. You throw a grapnel—a small hooked anchor—attached to a rope over the deck of the big ship. It bites into the wood. You and the crew shinny up the rope and stream on deck. You easily overpower the few wet, sleepy guards who have been left there. Then you batten down the hatches and nail shut the doors to below-decks, making the crew of the *Tremulous* prisoners in their own hold.

The ship is yours. You, McGillicuddy, and the crew look at one another in astonishment. It was so easy! You spend the rest of the night celebrating.

The rain lets up in the morning and a thick fog rolls in. You set off for New Rochelle with the *Margaret* in tow. You will be able to present George Washington with not only your message, but a British warship as well!

The End

"Let's play it safe," you say, "and anchor up the Harlem River. We can wait and see what develops."

McGillicuddy turns the *Margaret* around, and you find a good spot to weigh anchor. You wait, but nothing happens. The storm clouds keep building, but the rain doesn't come.

Finally, late in the afternoon, you decide to abandon the sea route. "We may never get through Hell Gate," you tell McGillicuddy. "Put me ashore. I'll go the rest of the way by land."

"Aye," McGillicuddy agrees. "We're not gettin' very far this way, are we?"

The *Margaret* pulls into a little inlet, and you are let over the side. McGillicuddy and the crew wave good-bye and wish you luck as you wade to the east shore. You plunge into the woods and head for the road north.

Turn to page 42.

You start backing down the cliff. But it's a lot easier to go up than down. You look over your shoulder to get an idea of where you're going. Several figures are gathered at the bottom. You start to turn around so you can descend frontward. Suddenly you lose your footing and slide down the rock gully!

You open your eyes, and immediately want to close them again. There is a pounding in your head like a jackhammer, and your limbs feel as if they've been mashed. You sit up, surprised to find nothing is broken. You are scraped and bruised all over, but otherwise intact.

Then you see the Mohawk watching you. He jumps up and returns with another Indian. This one kneels down and says, "You hurt?"

You nod.

"Here," he says, handing you a gourd. "Drink."

You take a drink from the gourd. The liquid makes you feel much better. The Indian waits for you to finish it, then introduces himself. "Call me M."

"M?"

"Yes, M—short for a name you can't pronounce." Then he says, "You will come with us now."

If you agree to go with him, turn to page 88.

If you say you want to stay, turn to page 110.

You and the crew hold the *Margaret* in the cove for as long as you dare. Finally the wind smooths out. An ominous quiet settles over the water. You move forward, but already the first gray light of dawn is filtering through the clouds. Yet you can see only the dim outlines of things around you. A gray wall looms ahead of you. Then you realize what is happening: You are in the middle of a thick fog.

The fog keeps rolling in from the Sound, growing heavier all the time, enveloping you.

You creep forward in the silence. No one on the *Margaret* says anything. Disembodied voices come out of nowhere, sounding very close, then are gone again. You can't tell how close the *Tremulous* is.

McGillicuddy revives after a while and helps you feel your way forward along the coast. You are startled when New Rochelle suddenly appears out of the fog. You've made it! The crew gives you a cheer as the *Margaret* pulls into the dock. McGillicuddy will find you a fast horse. From here it is only a half-day's ride to the American lines.

The End

You set down the harpoon, pick up a piece of wood, and resume paddling.

Soon another shape looms out of the fog. It's the *Tremulous*. Though heavily damaged, it can still sail. They spot you and come about. There is little you can do to escape. You and the crew are taken aboard, where you face the captain of the *Tremulous*.

"It's a pity your schooner escaped in the fog," he says. "We could have used more deckhands. His Majesty's Navy has a terrible manpower problem. Bloody nuisance fighting the rebels, you know."

He inspects you as you all stand in a line in your ragged clothes. Then he smiles and adds, "As you can see, there's quite a bit of repair work to be done around here. You look like you'll make good sailors."

Immediately you are put to work fixing the damaged rigging of the *Tremulous*. You have been impressed into the British Navy!

The End

The whale submerges. You lift the harpoon and wait.

"Thar she blows!" cries one of the crew, pointing behind you. You turn, take aim, and throw the harpoon. It's a perfect hit!

Spurred by the harpoon, the whale dives and swims off. The *Margaret* is dragged along behind it by the whale line attached to the harpoon.

"Whoo-ee!" yells McGillicuddy. "We're going for a Nantucket sleighride!"

The whale zigzags across the water, and you hold on for dear life. It seems the *Margaret* will be torn apart, but somehow she holds together. The wild ride lasts until noon. Finally the fog burns off and you sight land. You cut the harpoon rope and manage to paddle to shore.

"Where are we?" McGillicuddy asks a passing farmer when you reach a road. He looks at you as if you're from another planet. "Rhode Island!" he says, and walks off.

It's not exactly the route you planned. But if you borrow a fast horse from a nearby patriot, you should be able to get the message to George Washington in time.

The End

M helps you hobble to his canoe, moored on the bank of the Hudson. The rest of his party includes five more Mohawks, each with a canoe. They have two empty canoes in tow. Only later in the morning, as they paddle you down the Hudson, do you find out where they are going.

"We are going to see our English friends," M tells you. "We have just made an alliance with them. They are going to give us supplies."

This doesn't sound very good to you. "What about me?" you ask.

"You are injured. We will take you to an English hospital at their base on Staten Island."

An English hospital is the last place you want to be! Should you explain to M that you don't want to be involved with the English? Or should you keep quiet about that and look for a chance to escape in one of the empty canoes?

If you say you don't want to go to Staten Island, turn to page 76.

If you keep quiet, turn to page 92.

You quickly tell John you do not want to join up with him. "I think we have a better chance of escaping if we separate," you explain.

There is no time to wait for an answer. The British are coming. You dash off to the north. "Don't go that way!" you hear John yelling after you as you crash through the bushes.

Five minutes later you find out why—you've run right into a second search party coming down from King's Bridge. They collar you and haul you back to the outpost at the bridge. They have caught John too.

"I wasn't doing anything wrong!" you protest.

"Oh, no?" the British captain in charge of the manhunt says. "I suppose you were running through the woods for your health. Do you know what the penalty is for aiding a deserter?"

You soon find out—it is death.

The End

You turn your horse around to the right, splash across the stream, and crash into the thick woods. It is difficult going. The moonlight trickles through in only a few places, casting tangled shadows, and branches constantly grab at you and your horse.

You pause in your uphill climb after a while and listen for sounds of pursuit. There are none. You breathe a little easier. Perhaps you have finally shaken off the strange-looking rider.

You crest the hill and come into a clearing. Stopping for a moment to get your bearings, you notice a wooden blockhouse on the far side of the clearing. Suddenly the cold steel of a bayonet presses into your back. A harsh voice garbles some words at you. You raise your arms slowly and turn in your saddle.

The man holding the bayonet is a bizarre sight in the moonlight. He wears a bright green uniform trimmed in red and a cocked hat. A long greased ponytail hangs down his back, and his handlebar mustache is waxed to two sharp points. He is a Hessian grenadier—one of the German mercenaries for the British. You've escaped right into the hands of an enemy patrol!

Turn to page 95.

You don't say anything about the British to M. Biding your time, you travel down the Hudson with the Mohawks. They stop on the Jersey shore late in the afternoon.

You say you want to stay in the canoe because you don't think you can move with your injuries.

"Okay," M says. "We'll be right back."

You wait until they're out of sight, then you grab a couple of paddles and move to an empty canoe.

However, you have not seen the last of the Mohawks. A few miles downstream, just when you think you've escaped for sure, M and his friends suddenly appear in pursuit. You try to paddle faster, but soon you realize you are no match for them as a canoeist. They will catch up in a matter of minutes.

Your only hope is to go ashore. The Hoboken landing is just ahead. You pull in, spring onto the dock, and go as fast as you can into town. But that is not very fast. Your body still smarts from your fall from the Palisades.

A woman in Quaker dress sees you limping along the street. She watches you go by, then calls after you, "Is thee in need of help?"

You stop, turn, and hesitate for a moment before saying, "Yes—I'm being chased by Mohawks."

"Mohawks!"

You point down to the landing, where the Indians are tying up their canoes and looking your way. Without a word she grabs you by the arm and takes you down a side alley to her house.

Turn to page 102.

"Help!" you cry. "I'm a prisoner of the Mohawks! Help!"

M clamps his hand over your mouth and holds you down in the canoe. The men in blue don't notice you. The canoes glide silently up river. You've missed your last chance.

It takes only a few more days to carry the canoes and supplies over the mountains to the Delaware River and paddle up to M's town. It is surrounded by a high wall of pointed wooden poles. You are paraded through the gate with your hands bound behind your back. The people of the clan gather along the road to cheer the returning warriors. They jeer at you and heap abuse on your body, which is part of the ritual torture all captives receive. During the next few days, while the Mohawks celebrate with war dances, you are left up on a scaffold for all to ridicule.

Finally you are brought into one of the longhouses by an old woman. The elder women of the tribe, who make most of the important behind-the-scenes decisions, are holding council there. They summon M to translate.

"They say the hour of decision has come," M tells you. "They have one question for you."

"What is it?" you ask wearily.

"You may join our tribe—but are you willing to fight for the Mohawk cause?"

If you say yes, turn to page 101.

If you say no, turn to page 97.

You grab a loose rock and hurl it at the wolves at the top of the cliff. That frightens them a bit, and you climb up and pull yourself over the top. The wolves are still there, ten feet back, growling and looking very hungry. You let out a bloodcurdling yell and rush at them with a stick. They scatter, and you run off in the opposite direction.

Once you're sure you've shaken off the wolves, you head north through the woods, along the top of the Palisades. You figure eventually you will come across a road and will be able to get directions on a route to Haverstraw.

You walk all day, but no road appears. Darkness falls, and with it comes a heavy thunderstorm. You take shelter in a cave for the night—not realizing you are invading someone's home.

The inhabitant returns later in the night. You smell it first, then you hear its deep growl. Before you can get up, the grizzly bear has you trapped in the cave. You are dessert.

The End

The Hessian comes alongside you, keeping his bayonet disturbingly close to your body. You eye each other warily.

"I got lost in the woods," you say, and proceed to pour out your story about going to visit your uncle. You know he can't understand a word of it and hope it will confuse him.

"Quiet!" he snarls at you, then says some more words in German. He tries to make you move forward to the blockhouse.

"I can't," you insist, gesturing back toward the woods. "I must go that way. I'm late. They're waiting for me." Then you have an idea. You could say you are a courier for General Howe, the head of the British Army.

It's a risky proposition. A big lie could get you into a lot of trouble, but it might also fool the grenadier. On the other hand it might be safer to stick to the story about going to visit your uncle.

If you say General Howe is waiting for you, turn to page 100.

If you stick to the story about visiting your uncle, turn to page 111.

You hoist sail and move out. Almost instantly the wind grabs you and pulls you to the south. You and the crew struggle desperately to maintain an easterly course, but the wind tears at the sails. A big gust hits and you hear a loud crack. The mast comes crashing to the deck, split in half like a toothpick.

The crew takes to the oars, but they can do little against the current. You are carried helplessly across the Sound toward the south shore. Even after McGillicuddy comes to, he can't reverse your direction. The only consolation is that you aren't blown into the guns of the *Tremulous*.

Without warning, the *Margaret* runs aground on a sandbar. You are stopped short. But the water is shallow, so you and the crew are able to wade to shore. Wet and cold, you find shelter in a farmer's house on Long Island.

You have lost a day, but you may still be able to get the message to George Washington—you just hope you won't be too late. Only this time you'll take the land route.

The End

You shake your head no. It is only then that you learn *Mohawk* is an Algonquian word meaning "man-eater." It is the custom of the Mohawks to eat enemy warriors in order to get their strength.

That night you are slowly roasted over the fire and ceremonially consumed, piece by piece.

The End

"I still believe in the Revolution," you say firmly. "Something exciting is happening. I'm not exactly sure what it is, but I want to be part of it."

Amanda sighs. "I am a pacifist," she says. "I will not turn thee over to the British. I will not even prevent thee from leaving. But I wish thee would think about what I've said."

"I will," you promise. "Thank you for helping me. You've shown me there are thoughtful people on both sides."

You hurry off to complete your mission. If you can find a horse, there is still time for you to succeed.

The End

You look blankly at General Howe. "I haven't the faintest idea what you're talking about."

He looks at you for a moment. Then he folds his hands under his chin and raises the stakes.

"You know," he says thoughtfully, "it's obvious to everyone the American colonies don't stand a chance in this war. The sooner we end it, the fewer lives will be lost. We'll all make up and be friends again, and life will go back to normal." He leans forward. "In addition to putting yourself in a better position after the war ends, you would be doing your people a greater service by helping the Empire end this senseless war. Why not join our side? We pay double agents well."

The idea is preposterous. Unless . . . maybe you could *pretend* to become a double agent in order to escape.

On the other hand General Howe may still be bluffing.

If you say you'll become a double agent,
turn to page 104.

If you call General Howe's bluff again,
turn to page 108.

"General Howe is waiting for me," you tell the Hessian. "I'm a courier."

His ears perk up. *"Ja?"* he says. "General Howe?"

"Ja," you reply, nodding seriously. "General Howe *himself.*" The Hessian nods vigorously along with you. He tilts his head toward the blockhouse and says something about *der Kommandant.* You try to pull away, but in the end his bayonet convinces you to go to the blockhouse.

Apparently you are an important enough visitor to awaken the commandant. After he hears the grenadier's explanations, he turns to you with a smile and says, "So you are on business for General Howe? And you got lost in the woods?"

"Uh—yes," you say, trying to sound decisive.

"Well, then, it would be my honor to escort you personally to the general's quarters."

"Oh, no, that won't be necessary," you protest.

"Oh, but I insist," he says.

You remain silent. You don't want to draw suspicion by protesting any further.

The precious hours tick away as the Hessians escort you down the Bloomingdale Road and back into New York City. You have no chance to escape. It is morning by the time you get to the general's fashionable house on Broadway. The Hessians deposit you in the general's drawing room, where you are finally left alone.

This is the last place you expected to be! You are about to make a break for the door when the general comes into the room.

Turn to page 112.

"Yes, I will fight for the Mohawk cause," you say.

The women smile and congratulate you. As is their custom, the Mohawks adopt you as one of their own. You take the place of a warrior who was killed in battle. You learn the Mohawk ways and come to share their awe for the forces of the universe.

Eventually the Revolution comes to an end. But the fighting is not over for you. You find yourself battling the newly independent colonists, your former compatriots, as they break treaties and try to take over Mohawk land. As a Mohawk, you are not so sure independence is the greatest thing for America.

The End

"Thee will be safe here," the Quaker woman says as she sets a tray of herb tea and muffins in front of you. "My name is Amanda. I have just one question for thee: Why are the Mohawks chasing thee?"

"They want to make me their captive," you explain. "They have joined the British side."

She nods slowly and says, "So thee is one of the rebels?"

You see now that it was a mistake to assume she was on your side. But there's no going back now. "Yes," you say.

She is silent for a while. You eat a muffin. Finally she says, "I do not support thy cause. I do not see any need for armed rebellion. We can solve our differences by talk, not by force."

"But the English used force first," you object. "As long as they held the threat of force over us, they would never really listen to us."

Amanda shakes her head. "There are some good men in the British government. They would have listened. I think America has been led astray by a few rabble-rousers and hothead rebel leaders. If they win, we will only have chaos."

You fear that if you stick to your beliefs, Amanda will turn you over to the British. What should you say?

*If you say, "I still believe in the Revolution,"
turn to page 98.*

*If you say "I think you are right" to Amanda,
turn to page 105.*

104

You act as if you were weighing General Howe's offer. After a momentous pause you say, "You're right. I'll become a double agent."

The general stands up and smiles. "Good. A wise move." He fishes a snuffbox out of a bag hanging at his side and puts some of the powder up his nose. His sneeze rings with satisfaction.

"Now," he says, dabbing his nose with a lace handkerchief, "let's have a look at your plans."

You didn't foresee this. You ask yourself if he really does know about the plans. If so, refusal to cooperate would betray your purpose. Your career as a double agent—and as an agent—would be a short one indeed. Yet if he doesn't know about them, turning them over would mean disaster.

If you play the double agent to the hilt and give him the envelope, turn to page 109.

If you assure him that you aren't carrying any plans, turn to page 114.

"I think you are right," you say to Amanda.

"Good," she says. "Now wait right here. I know a British agent who can help thee."

"Wait!" you call.

But Amanda is already out the door. You hurriedly begin to gather up your gear. Your only hope is to leave before Amanda gets back, even though your escape from the Mohawks has weakened you.

You just make it to the door when Amanda bursts in with a burly gentleman. She sees your gear in your hands and says, "Good, thee is ready to go. This is Mr. Quisenberry. He will take thee to New York. Maybe he will even be able to get thee a position in British intelligence!"

Trying to look cheerful, you load your stuff into the waiting buckboard. Perhaps you will have a chance to escape from Mr. Quisenberry on the way to New York. But you doubt it.

The End

You start rocking the canoe. M looks back at you in midpaddle and says, "What are you doing?"

A few more rocks and the canoe goes over. You manage to grab the canoe beside you and tip it over too. This creates chaos as you all splash around in the water. You swim for the riverbank. The Mohawks pursue, but you kick water in their faces.

The commotion attracts the attention of the soldiers marching by. A man on a horse comes crashing through the bushes and into the water. At the sight of him the Indians give up the chase and escape in their canoes.

The man helps you on the back of his horse and takes you to safety. Only then do you discover you have been rescued by George Washington!

Back at the American camp you give General Washington the envelope, and he sends you off to get some dry clothes. After you enjoy a good meal with the American Army, the general calls you into his tent.

"As you can see," he says, "we're on our way to Philadelphia already. It would have been nice to have this information a few days ago so we could have gotten a jump on the British. But the plans will still help us. How would you like to join my espionage staff?"

The End

You spread your hands. "I'm just a simple farmer. I really don't understand all this talk."

General Howe looks at you for a long time. "Why are you here, then?"

You shrug. "I don't know. They picked me up in the woods. They must have mistaken me for someone else."

Howe abruptly stands up and rings for his servant. The general ignores you completely as you are led out of the drawing room.

The British confiscate your horse before they let you go. They tell you it has been officially appropriated for the war effort. There is nothing you can do about it, so you go back to Ephraim's stable. He outfits you with a new horse, and you take off northward—late, but not too late to complete your journey.

The End

You try to show no hesitation about removing the letter from your boot. You hand it to General Howe, who accepts it with a bow and rings for his aide.

"Bring in the guards," he orders the aide, tapping the envelope on his desk with gratification. "We have a spy to be taken to the stockade. I expect we shall also have a hanging soon."

You've been tricked. As you are led away you start to object, but General Howe has already forgotten you.

The End

"No," you say to the Mohawk, "I can't go with you. I—" But you are unable to think up an excuse.

"You are weak and probably will not survive," he replies. "But you make the decision. We will leave you."

He brings your blanket and saddlebag; then the Mohawks move off down the river in their canoes. Now that you are alone, you feel a twinge of regret.

Your regret gets bigger when you realize you cannot travel today. You need at least one day of rest to recover from your fall.

You sink into sleep. An insistent buzzing awakes you. A horde of mosquitoes is gathered above your head, thick as a thundercloud. How ridiculous, you think as delirium overtakes you, to be finished off by mosquitoes.

The End

You are put under guard for the rest of the night. In the morning you are brought in to see the commandant.

"What were you doing out last night?" he asks sharply.

"I got lost in the woods," you explain. "I was going to visit my uncle."

"At three in the morning?"

"Yes. It's a long way," you say.

"What's the rush?"

"Well, he's sick and doesn't have anyone to take care of him."

The commandant eyes you for a minute before coming to a decision. "We can't take any risks," he says. "The British troops are making some important movements in the next three days. We will hold you here under guard until they are finished. I'm sorry, but your uncle will have to wait."

So will George Washington.

The End

112

"Would you like a cup of tea?" General Howe asks after he has seated himself at his desk.

His hospitality takes you aback a bit. You accept the cup and saucer from his servant.

The general sits down at his desk and savors his tea. You can't help being impressed by his aristocratic features and suave manner.

"Beastly war," he comments. "Personally I think the rebels have got a good point. But why must we resolve our differences by arms? It seems such a waste."

"Yes," you say, searching for a suitably neutral comment. "Civil war is a terrible thing."

The general places his cup on the desk. "Now, why don't you come clean. We know what you're up to. Hand over the plans."

His voice is so cool and easy that the meaning of his words doesn't immediately sink in. As you consider it he picks up his teacup and before taking a sip, adds casually, "It'd be a pity for you to hang."

There's a window behind you. You could make a break for it, but that would give you away. Perhaps you should just pretend you don't know what General Howe is talking about.

If you say nothing and try to make a break for the window, turn to page 115.

If you say you don't know what General Howe is talking about, turn to page 99.

"There are no plans," you tell General Howe with as much certainty as you can muster.

"Very well." General Howe sighs. "We must trust each other, I suppose." He sits down at his desk and writes out a letter.

"Now you have some plans to take to Mr. Washington," he says, sealing the letter with his stamp and handing it to you. "I'm sure he will find the information useful." He allows a little smile to turn up the corners of his mouth.

"When do I get paid?" you ask.

He waves his hand toward the door. "My aide will take care of all that. You get paid when you bring back some intelligence of value."

Your horse is brought out and you gallop away to a career as a *double* double agent.

The End

You say nothing to General Howe. How, you wonder, did he find out? Someone in the rebel network must be a double agent, you decide.

General Howe rings for his guards. You race to the window, open it, and jump out. But it only leads into a courtyard! General Howe yells instructions to his men in the courtyard, and soon they collar you. You are brought back inside to stand before the general.

"Don't make us do unpleasant things," Howe says. "Hand over the plans now."

With resignation you give him the envelope. Howe takes a moment to read it. A puzzled look comes over his face briefly. Then he sets it down and says sharply, "Now I want names. Who are the rebel spies in New York?"

"I'll never tell," you declare.

"Very well," he replies. "We'll put you aboard our prison ship. I'm sure after a few weeks in that miserable place, you'll change your mind."

The End

ABOUT THE FACTS IN THIS BOOK

Many of the adventures in *Spy for George Washington* are based on actual historical events and almost all the characters are based on historical figures or types.

In mid-July 1777 George Washington marched through New Jersey to a position near Haverstraw on the Hudson River. There he waited for a few days, poised for the British to move to Albany. But General Howe went for Philadelphia instead, in a decision that is still questioned today.

If you had been an agent a year later, in 1778, the information about this move could have been obtained and transmitted through a well-established New York and Long Island spy network—and probably would have been transmitted in the form of an invisible-ink letter in the manner described. But in 1777 the American spy network was in its infancy, which is why you had so little help on your journey to Haverstraw.

There was more than one New York–based plot to kidnap or assassinate George Washington; there was also a maid in Westchester who freed an American agent by drugging her master. American whaleboat captains undertook astonishingly daring raids, and most of the adventures with McGillicuddy are based on true stories. The descriptions of your treatment at the hands of the Mohawks are based on Jesuit accounts of captivity. While General Howe's demeanor has been imagined, it was not unusual for the British to try to recruit American double agents, nor was it unusual for them to force a runaway slave like John into their army.

ABOUT THE AUTHOR

JAY LEIBOLD was born in Denver, Colorado, and now lives in San Francisco, California. He has also written *Sabotage* and *Grand Canyon Odyssey* for the Choose Your Own Adventure series and is working on a new book about parallel universes.

ABOUT THE ILLUSTRATOR

DON HEDIN was the first artist for the Choose Your Own Adventure series, working under the name of Paul Granger, and has illustrated over twenty-five books for the series. For many years, Mr. Hedin was associated with *Reader's Digest* as a staff illustrator and then art editor. With his wife, who is also an artist, Mr. Hedin now lives in Oak Creek Canyon, Arizona, where he continues to work as a fine-arts painter and illustrator.

BANTAM
SHOP-AT-HOME
C·A·T·A·L·O·G

Special Offer
Buy a Bantam Book
for only 50¢.

Now you can have Bantam's catalog filled with hundreds of titles plus take advantage of our unique and exciting bonus book offer. A special offer which gives you the opportunity to purchase a Bantam book for only 50¢. Here's how!

By ordering any five books at the regular price per order, you can also choose any other single book listed (up to a $5.95 value) for just 50¢. Some restrictions do apply, but for further details why not send for Bantam's catalog of titles today!

Just send us your name and address and we will send you a catalog!

BANTAM BOOKS, INC.
P.O. Box 1006, South Holland, Ill. 60473

Mr./Mrs./Ms. _____
(please print)

Address _____

City _____ State _____ Zip _____

FC(A)—10/87

Please allow four to six weeks for delivery.